First published in Great Britain in 2002 by Brimax,
an imprint of Octopus Publishing Group Ltd
2-4 Heron Quays, London E14 4JP
© Octopus Publishing Group Ltd

3 5 7 9 10 8 6 4 2

ISBN 1 85854 363 0

Printed in China

A CIP catalogue record for this book is available
from the British Library.

Schooltime for Sammy

BRIMAX

While his brother and sister got ready for the first
day of school, Sammy was busy playing. He climbed
his favourite tree and swung from branch to branch.
Pushing books into his satchel, Fred called up,
"You're old enough to go to school this year, Sammy."
"I don't want to go to school!
I want to stay home and play!" replied Sammy.

"But school is fun, and you'll learn all
kinds of things," said Sophie.
"I'm not going!" said Sammy, dangling upside
down and pulling a face. "I already know
everything. I know how to climb all the tallest
trees and I can swing really fast.
So there! Catch me if you can!"
But Fred and Sophie didn't chase after him –
they didn't want to be late for school.

Sammy spent the morning playing but soon
got bored without any playmates.
"What's wrong, Sammy?" asked his mother,
when she found him moping.
"There's nobody to play with," said Sammy grumpily.
"Well, your friends are all at school," explained
his mum. "Maybe you should go, too."
"No way!" shouted Sammy,
scrambling back up the tree.

At last, Sophie and Fred returned home,
chattering excitedly about their busy day. Sammy
ran to greet them with an after-school snack.

Sammy wanted Fred and Sophie to play with him,
but they said that they had homework to do.
Sammy did not want to be left out.
"I can do homework," he said, climbing onto
a chair and joining them at the table.
"How many days are there in April?" Fred asked Sophie.
"Twenty five ninety zillion!" shouted Sammy, trying to help.
"Oh, Sammy, don't be silly. We're trying to work,"
said Sophie with a sigh.

When Sammy's friend Jack came to visit,
he was full of news about his new school.
"The teacher is really nice and I've learned lots
of important things," said Jack proudly.
"I know what two plus one plus two is."
"So do I!" said Sammy,
trying to count on his fingers.
"What is it, then?" asked Jack.
"It's, um, it's... a lot!" he answered.
"You don't know!" exclaimed Jack.

Now Sammy was quite curious about school.
"What else did you do at school, Jack?" he asked.
"Well, I made lots of new friends and we
all played games together," said Jack.

As Sammy listened, Jack told him everything
that he had learned. His favourite part of the day
was Show and Tell, when people could bring in
special things and share them with the class.
"You really did do a lot,"
said Sammy with a sad sigh.

That night at dinner, Sammy was very quiet.
He did not even feel like eating his dinner.
Nobody noticed, though, because Sophie and Fred
were chattering loudly about school.
"I got a gold star on my spelling test," bragged Sophie.
"I won a race at playtime," said Fred proudly.
"Well done, both of you," said their mother and father.

The next morning, Sammy woke up very early.
He was very excited as he searched for the
little satchel that his mother had made for him.
When he found it, he packed Effalump,
his favourite toy, carefully inside.
He wanted to have something for Show and Tell.
Sammy marched into the kitchen
and announced, "I'm ready!"

Sammy's family looked up in surprise.
"Ready for what, Sammy?" asked his father.
"I want to go to school after all," declared
Sammy. "I want to learn how to read and write
and count and draw beautiful pictures."
"That's wonderful," said his mother.
"But first you'll need to have some breakfast."

After breakfast, Sammy set off with Sophie
and Fred, walking at a very quick pace.
"I'm already a day late for school," said Sammy
with a grin. "I don't want to miss any more!"